Internet Safety

Internet Safety

Josepha Sherman

Watts LIBRARY™

Franklin Watts
A Division of Scholastic Inc.
New York • Toronto • London • Auckland • Sydney
Mexico City • New Delhi • Hong Kong
Danbury, Connecticut

Note to readers: Definitions for words in **bold** can be found in the Glossary at the back of this book.

Library of Congress Cataloging-in-Publication Data

Sherman, Josepha.
    Internet Safety / by Josepha Sherman.
        p. cm — (Watts library)
    Summary: Provides information and advice on using the Internet safely, discussing privacy concerns, viruses, shopping online, netiquette, and more.
    Includes bibliographical references and index.
    ISBN 0-531-12165-8 (lib. bdg.)   0-531-16212-5 (pbk.)
    1. Internet—History—Juvenile literature. [1. Internet—History.] I. Title. II. Series.
TK5105.875.I57 S522 2003
004.67′8—dc21

2002008506

Contents

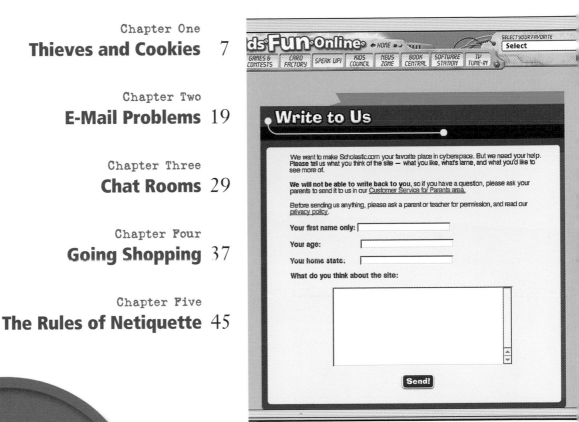

The Internet offers numerous opportunities to learn about new things and interact with people from around the world.

Chapter One

Thieves and Cookies

If you've spent any time at all online, you know that the Internet is a truly wonderful creation. Among the many things you can do online is go shopping in all sorts of Internet stores, see artwork from museums in many countries, and keep in touch with your friends and, indeed, with much of the world. You can hear music, learn about science, and even watch Space Station Alpha, the International Space Station, being built. You can also

Document Title: NASA Information Services via World Wide W

Document URL: http://www.gsfc.nasa.gov/NASA_homepage.htm

National Aeronautics and Space Administration

National Aeronautics and
Space Administration

World Wide Web (WWW) information services

* Hot Topics * .... NASA news and subjects of public interest

NASA's Strategic Plan, Specific NASA Strategies & Policies

NASA Public Affairs

NASA Educational Programs, NASA Online Educational Resources

NASA Information Sources by Subject

NASA Centers (click on a center's name for its home page):

Back | Forward | Home | Reload | Open... | Save As... | Clone | New Window | Close Window

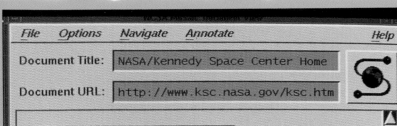

File	Options	Navigate	Annotate		Help

Document Title: NASA/Kennedy Space Center Home

Document URL: http://www.ksc.nasa.gov/ksc.htm

NASA Kennedy Space Center Home Page

Welcome to KSC's World Wide Web (WWW) information center. From this document, you can access a variety of useful information at the Kennedy Space Center. You can find out What's New on KSC's server, or Hot Topics within NASA or Other Important Announcements.

- About Kennedy Space Center
- Facilities at KSC
- Historical Archive
- Shuttle Mission Information
- Shuttle Reference Manual
- Frequently Asked Questions
- Search for Information
- KSC Gopher server
- KSC X.500 Locator Service

Next Shuttle Mission

Back	Forward	Home	Reload	Open...	Save As...	Clone	New Window

The Crowded Frontier

National Aeronautics and Space Administration (NASA) space missions have become so popular that it's sometimes difficult to get on to NASA's website. Whenever there is a new launch or a new discovery, NASA often has to put up a mirror, or duplicate, site so that everyone can see what is happening.

You probably encounter forms all the time at school.

attend classes online. But, as in any other community, there are certain facts you need to know about life in the Internet community if you are going to have a good time online and avoid any of the possible dangers.

Possible Online Hazards

Think about the problems of theft and spying. At this point, you may be wondering what these issues have to do with the Internet. Aren't you safe from thieves and spies when you are using the Internet? After all, this isn't a cartoon world. No one's going to reach out of the computer screen to snatch your wallet.

While no one can physically take anything away from you over the Internet, your identity, or who you are, is in danger every time you surf the Internet. And it is easy not to see that danger until it is too late. For example, many sites ask you to register with them by filling out a form. You probably have gotten used to filling out forms. You probably fill out forms in school so often that you do not really stop to think about what you are doing.

However, when you are online, it is very important to be careful about the information you put into the forms you encounter. Before you give online companies any information, check to see why they want it. A **legitimate** company will state the reason clearly on its website. The company might need the information to ship you something you bought or to make

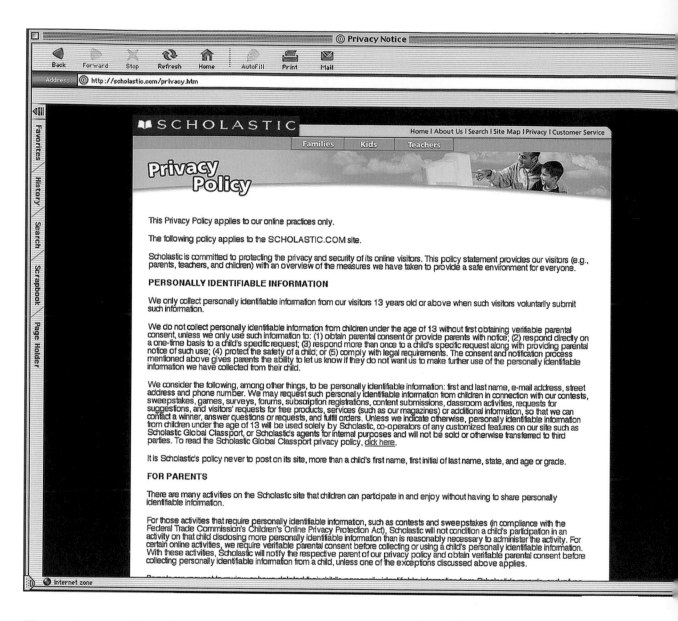

SCHOLASTIC

Home I About Us I Search I Site Map I Privacy I Customer Service

Families   Kids   Teachers

Privacy Policy

This Privacy Policy applies to our online practices only.

The following policy applies to the SCHOLASTIC.COM site.

Scholastic is committed to protecting the privacy and security of its online visitors. This policy statement provides our visitors (e.g., parents, teachers, and children) with an overview of the measures we have taken to provide a safe environment for everyone.

PERSONALLY IDENTIFIABLE INFORMATION

We only collect personally identifiable information from our visitors 13 years old or above when such visitors voluntarily submit such information.

We do not collect personally identifiable information from children under the age of 13 without first obtaining verifiable parental consent, unless we only use such information to: (1) obtain parental consent or provide parents with notice; (2) respond directly on a one-time basis to a child's specific request; (3) respond more than once to a child's specific request along with providing parental notice of such use; (4) protect the safety of a child; or (5) comply with legal requirements. The consent and notification process mentioned above gives parents the ability to let us know if they do not want us to make further use of the personally identifiable information we have collected from their child.

We consider the following, among other things, to be personally identifiable information: first and last name, e-mail address, street address and phone number. We may request such personally identifiable information from children in connection with our contests, sweepstakes, games, surveys, forums, subscription registrations, content submissions, classroom activities, requests for suggestions, and visitors' requests for free products, services (such as our magazines) or additional information, so that we can contact a winner, answer questions or requests, and fulfill orders. Unless we indicate otherwise, personally identifiable information from children under the age of 13 will be used solely by Scholastic, co-operators of any customized features on our site such as Scholastic Global Classport, or Scholastic's agents for internal purposes and will not be sold or otherwise transferred to third parties. To read the Scholastic Global Classport privacy policy, click here.

It is Scholastic's policy never to post on its site, more than a child's first name, first initial of last name, state, and age or grade.

FOR PARENTS

There are many activities on the Scholastic site that children can participate in and enjoy without having to share personally identifiable information.

For those activities that require personally identifiable information, such as contests and sweepstakes (in compliance with the Federal Trade Commission's Children's Online Privacy Protection Act), Scholastic will not condition a child's participation in an activity on that child disclosing more personally identifiable information than is reasonably necessary to administer the activity. For certain online activities, we require verifiable parental consent before collecting or using a child's personally identifiable information. With these activities, Scholastic will notify the respective parent of our privacy policy and obtain verifiable parental consent before collecting personally identifiable information from a child, unless one of the exceptions discussed above applies.

Internet zone

This web page explains the site's policies regarding your privacy. It advises visitors that it will not collect information from children under age thirteen without parental permission.

sure your membership in a club is recorded. They might need the information as part of a marketing survey.

Before you fill out that form, even if there

seems to be a good reason for doing it, you should also check to see if there is a **guarantee** of **privacy** somewhere on the site. That guarantee is a promise that the company owning the site will keep your information only for its own use, and won't sell the lists of names and addresses taken from these forms to other companies.

Here is another problem with forms. Not only are you used to filling out forms, you are used to filling them out completely—whether it is necessary or not. Take a look at an online form and you will see that you are being asked to fill in only some of the lines. Sometimes these lines are marked with a symbol or appear in a different color. Do not give people you don't know information about yourself that they don't actually need. If you have any doubts about what information should and should not be filled in, always ask your parents.

There can be many different consequences if you do fill out all the lines on an online form without thinking about why you are doing it or checking for a guarantee of privacy. At the very least, if the owners of the site do not post their privacy policy, your name and address could be added to a list sold to junk mail companies. This means lots of junk mail will fill up your mailbox. A more serious consequence of giving out too much personal information would be having your name and identity used without your knowledge. Someone might use it to buy things you never ordered or to send someone else threatening letters in your name.

Address: http://scholastic.com/kids/write.asp

Kids Fun Online ← HOME

GAMES & CONTESTS | CARD FACTORY | SPEAK UP! | KIDS COUNCIL | NEWS ZONE | BOOK CENTRAL | SOFTWARE STATION | TV TUNE-IN

SELECT YOUR FAVORITE
Select

GO

Write to Us

We want to make Scholastic.com your favorite place in cyberspace. But we need your help. Please tell us what you think of the site — what you like, what's lame, and what you'd like to see more of.

We will not be able to write back to you, so if you have a question, please ask your parents to send it to us in our Customer Service for Parents area.

Before sending us anything, please ask a parent or teacher for permission, and read our privacy policy.

Your first name only:

Your age:

Your home state:

What do you think about the site:

Send!

Internet zone

This form asks for visitors to send in their reactions to the website. Notice how it mentions getting permission before sending any information.

Electronic Cookies

Another problem involves cookies. Internet cookies are not of the edible variety. In computer terms, a cookie is a small piece of computer text. It is usually made up of a string of random letters. Often when you visit a site, such as

14

Online companies, such as Amazon.com, may use cookies to remember who you are and what kinds of things you like.

Watch Out!

Be wary of any e-mails you receive asking about your account information. You may get an e-mail that looks like it is from your **Internet Service Provider** (ISP) that says that your account information needs to be updated or the credit card you signed up with is invalid or expired and the information needs to be reentered to keep your account active. Never answer this type of e-mail, and do not give whoever sent it any credit card information. First contact your ISP to find out if the message is authentic. According to the U.S. Trade Commission, such an e-mail request could very well be a scam.

Amazon.com, an online bookstore, their **web server** stores a cookie on your computer's hard drive. If you look in your computer's browser directory, or folder, you will usually find them in a file called cookies, cookies.txt, or MagicCookie. In the case of a legitimate company, there is a good reason for cookies. A cookie identifies you to a website so that the website can retrieve your records from its web server system, take you straight to where you want to go on a site, or show you items that match your taste.

Unfortunately, not all websites are run by honest people. Some of the less honest ones use cookies to gather information about you. While the cookies themselves are not gathering that data, they can be used as tracking devices. If you look at your cookies file you may see the names of websites you don't recognize and that you know you haven't visited. These probably came from companies that sell advertising to other companies. They have huge files that keep track of who looks at which pages, when, and for how long. They can exchange this information and cookies with other companies. It's nobody's business where you go on the Internet, and it's certainly not right for someone to sell information about you without your knowledge or permission.

The best way to keep anyone online from learning too much about you, besides being careful about forms, is to regularly delete the cookies that accumulate on your hard drive. There are two ways that you can do this. One is to empty your web browser's cache, a virtual storage area on your hard drive.

A Case in Point

On May 21, 2002, an online advertising company called DoubleClick settled state and federal lawsuits that had charged it with violating users' privacy. Now DoubleClick must provide its users with a privacy policy that clearly explains its online services and its use of cookies. It also has to destroy its files of names, addresses, telephone numbers, and e-mail addresses. In addition, DoubleClick has to get permission from Internet users before it can link personal information with users' Internet histories.

If you are not sure how to do this, check with your Internet Service Provider (ISP)—the company that gives you access to the Internet—or ask your parents. You can also check with the companies that made the web browser you are using. You can also delete cookies and clean out your cache while online. Again, if you're not sure how to do this, check with your ISP or your parents. Think of it as an easy way to stop spies cold.

E-mail is a wonderful way to keep in touch with friends and family both far and near.

Chapter Two

E-Mail Problems

E-mail, as everyone who has ever used it is sure to agree, is one of the most amazing things about the Internet, as well as one of the most useful. You can stay in touch with all your friends through e-mail. You can send them photos of your new dog, or let your grandmother on the other side of the country read your prizewinning essay on the same day you won the prize. And during emergencies, such as the September 11 attack on the World Trade Center in New York City, it was e-mail that enabled friends around the world to find out almost instantly that loved ones were safe.

Fighting Viruses

Sadly, however, there always seem to be people who like to cause harm, and because of them, there is also a darker side to e-mail. E-mail can be used to spread **computer viruses**. A virus in humans is a microscopic agent that makes people sick. A computer virus is a program that someone has written out

The Melissa Virus

A few years ago, a computer virus called the Melissa virus spread through thousands of computers in the form of an e-mail message with an infected document as an attachment. The subject header of the e-mail was usually "Important Message From [name of the user sending the message]" and the message was often, "Here is that document you asked for ... don't show anyone else." When the attachment was opened, the virus infected the computer. The creator of the Melissa virus was caught by the Federal

Bureau of Investigation (FBI) and is serving time in prison.

to deliberately damage or even destroy the data stored in computers. Thousands of these viruses and **worms**—which are similar to computer viruses—exist in the computer world.

How does your computer catch a computer virus? One way is downloading a file off the Internet without running the file through an antivirus program, or virus checker, before opening it. Another way to catch a virus is by opening an e-mail attachment without running it through an antivirus software first. An attachment is a file that can be opened through a link in an e-mail message. Many computers have been infected through e-mail attachments opened by people who forgot to check them out first. Never open an attachment from anyone you don't know. And even if the attachment comes from someone you do know, it is still a good idea run a virus scan on the

Antivirus software can be set up to scan your e-mail for possible viruses.

Scan Result: **Virus *W32.Sircam.Worm@mm* found. File NOT cleaned.**

This file contains a computer worm, a program that spreads very quickly over the Internet to many computers and can delete files, steal sensitive information, or render your machine unusable.

This attachment has a virus that may infect your computer. It cannot be cleaned. We recommend that you DO NOT download this attachment.

attachment before opening it. There could be a virus on the other person's computer that he or she might not know about yet. In fact, you can set your antivirus program to scan attachments automatically. Another potential hiding place for viruses is on floppy disks and CDs so remember to scan anything you put in your computer before opening it.

There are several good antivirus programs available that will check for viruses and get rid of any that they find. The two most popular programs are Symantec's Norton Antivirus and McAfee's VirusScan. Both of these programs can be set up to download new virus definitions automatically. That way your computer will always have the latest information on how to handle even the newest viruses.

Spam in Your Inbox

Another e-mail problem that can be a real nuisance is **spam**. You have probably heard of Spam, the canned meat product, and maybe even seen cans of it on grocery store shelves. E-mail spam is named after that canned meat because it's as universal as Spam, which means that it is everywhere.

In short, computer spam is e-mail junk mail, and it has been flooding e-mail inboxes around the world for several years. Some spam really is just a nuisance and relatively harmless. It consists of advertisements, which are the online version of mail you don't want. E-mail ads that come from California and other states with laws regulating spam will read "AD" or

Spam is an electronic version of the junk mail many people get at home.

"Advertisement" in the heading. That way you know what it is right away, and can delete it unread.

Other spam senders aren't so honest. Suppose that you get an e-mail with "Long time no see!" or "Bet you don't remember me!" in the subject heading. The odds are pretty good that you never saw the first person at all, and you certainly don't remember the second person because you never met anyone with that e-mail address. And that is the clue right there. If you don't recognize the address, no matter how friendly the subject header might look, the e-mail is probably an advertising gimmick.

In addition to misleading subject headers, there's a whole list of e-mail scams. You might get an e-mail that reads "Click here for valuable prizes" or "Congratulations! You're a Winner!" Other spam senders may be more direct and write "Send money" or "Give us your credit card number."

You already may have seen some or all of these headings. These messages are most likely scams by people trying to get your money. Yes, it may be tempting to see what is hiding behind the spam, but don't do it. Never click on any links in an e-mail from someone you don't know. There have even been cases of a spam message that allowed the person sending it to pretend to be the computer user and charge long-distance telephone calls to the user. Nothing that bad may happen to you, but clicking on the link won't help you get rid of the spam, and you won't get anything good out of doing it, either.

If you have already had spam messages clog up your e-mail mailbox, you have probably gotten pretty angry. Take heart! You are not alone. In fact, so many people are angry that Congress has been considering passing laws to regulate spam.

What's the Word?

A password is a set of letters, numbers, and symbols that allows you to gain admission to a restricted place. A computer password gives you access to your Internet account or online shopping accounts. When you need to set a password, think first. If you make it a word that is easy for you to remember, someone else might be able to figure it out. For instance, if everyone knows that you are a baseball fan, don't make "World Series" your password. Don't use the names of your family members or pets, either, or anything else someone might know about you, such as your birthday. It's better to make up a password with letters, numbers, and symbols in it. A password like M2an$I32* might not look pretty, but it might keep your account safe. Don't forget! You'll need different passwords for each of your accounts.

Nothing has been decided yet. So, in the meantime, you could try to get off a spam list by clicking on the "remove from mailing list" link in the message. However, this sometimes backfires. Instead of removing you from the mailing list, responding to the spam message lets the sender know that they have reached an active e-mail address, and the sender may send more spam your way.

You might already have heard this warning, but it is worth repeating. Never, ever give out your password to anyone. That's just asking someone to take over your account!

One way to cut down on the number of spam e-mails you receive is to forward all spam you receive directly to your service provider. Be sure to include the headers and footers, or the material at the very top and bottom of the message. Sometimes you have to scroll down quite a way to find the footer, because whoever sent the e-mail doesn't want you to find it. The footer contains information that can be used to trace the spam back to its sender.

Getting Rid of Spam

Some companies, such as AOL, have departments set up to handle spam. An AOL user simply forwards the spam message to TOS SPAM. There are also online sites that have been created to help get rid of spam. The Coalition Against Unsolicited Commercial Email (CAUCE) is made up of volunteers trying to get Congress to solve the spam problem. Spam Cop, http://spamcop.net, is a site that will help you track down the source of the spam you receive.

If you receive any e-mail message that you find really nasty, you're under no obligation to answer it. In fact, don't answer it. Instead, contact your ISP immediately, or have your parents do it. If someone you don't know sends you what looks like a friendly, important, or just plain weird e-mail, don't answer that either. If you do, the sender learns that your e-mail address is "live," one that you actually use. If anyone, whether you know them or not, sends you a threat through e-mail, don't hesitate. Tell your parents right away, and contact your ISP.

It is important to let your parents know if you get any strange or threatening e-mail messages.

A chat room allows you to talk online with people from around the world.

Chapter Three

Chat Rooms

Chat rooms are online sites in which you can talk with other people in real time. This means the chat occurs at the present time without delays. People communicate with one another by typing and sending messages that appear on the screens of everyone "in" the chat room, almost as though you were actually in a room with them. There are chat rooms for almost every group of users who have a shared interest in something, from members of a club to fans of television programs or movies. If you can't find a chat room that matches your interests, you can even start your own.

Be Careful Where You Go

Chat rooms can be a lot of fun, if you know which ones to go into. Some of the open chat room sites are aimed at adults only and say so in their listings. You may think that it is daring to go into one of those sites. But if you do go into one of the adults-only chats, you'll find that it's not any fun, since no one in there is going to type about anything you want to read. And, of course, there is always the chance that you could get in a lot of trouble in one of the adults-only chat sites. Not everyone is a nice person and you might find yourself in over your head with an adult who knows you're a kid—and doesn't care. Besides, imagine what would happen if you ran into someone whom your parents know or if your parents happened to see what site you were visiting!

Once you find a chat room that's right for you, you still need to be careful. Unless you know everyone in the chat room personally, it's going to be difficult to be sure who's who. As a cartoon in *New Yorker* magazine once said, "On the Internet, no one knows that you're a dog." The computer only knows that you can type. You could be anyone!

Finding Chats

How do you find chat rooms you want to visit? One way is to search Yahooligans! The Web Guide for Kids, http://www.yahooligans.com/, which is the kids-only version of Yahoo! Another way is to go to Ask Jeeves for Kids, http://www.ajkids.com/, the kids-only version of AskJeeves.com. These will lead you to kids-only chat rooms.

It's impossible to know who is with you in a chat room. Suppose that you run into someone online who is using the screen name "Glitter." The screen name doesn't give you any real information. Glitter could be a girl or a boy, or even an

If you plan on visiting chat rooms, it's important not to reveal personal information online, such as who you are or where you live.

Know Before You Go

Private chats are just that—off-limits to anyone who does not have the right password. Unless someone you know invites you into a private chat, don't go. Why would a stranger invite you into a private chat unless he or she wanted to cause trouble for you?

adult pretending to be a kid. It is sad but true that there are some dangerous adults who are looking for girls or boys they can trick into meeting them.

Take Some Precautions

Not knowing who is behind the online names doesn't mean you will be in danger, as long as you use your head. There are a few commonsense precautions you can take. Don't log on under your own name. Most ISPs will let you log on under a made-up screen name. Pick a name that doesn't sound like it belongs to either a boy or a girl. Screen names, such as "Biker" or "Trekfan," don't tell someone too much about you.

You may find that someone in the chat room really, really wants to know how old you are or where you live, and may

Don't let anyone pressure you into providing information about yourself. If someone is bothering you, let your parents and your ISP know about the problem.

Energy Creatures

There are some people who like to go into chat rooms just to cause trouble. These are the ones who will start saying mean things, such as "Star Trek Stinks!" or calling everyone dirty names to make them angry. It is really tempting to tell a troublemaker like that what you think of him or her. But why waste your time and lose your temper? If the troublemaker is going to act like a baby screaming for attention, why would you want to give that troublemaker what he or she wants? There is a saying in online communities, "Don't feed the energy creature!" In other words, if you and every-

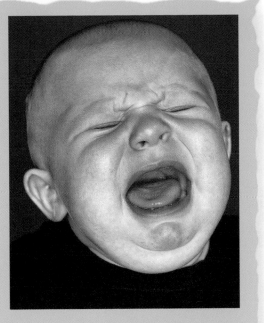

one else in the chat room simply ignore the troublemaker, pretty soon he or she will get frustrated and go away.

even be sending you private messages asking for that information. It may strike you as weird—and it is. Anything personal about you is not a stranger's business. So never volunteer your age or address, no matter how many times someone asks. In fact, if someone keeps asking, or insists on meeting you alone somewhere face-to-face, or in a private chat room, don't answer. This may just be a case of some kid being a nuisance. But it may also be someone trying to cause you harm. Instead of answering the nosy person, report the user right away to your service provider and your parents.

The advice about chat rooms also applies to Instant Messages (IM). An IM service is a way to send someone a real-time message, as though you and the person exchanging the IMs were in a private chat room. If you get an IM from someone you don't recognize, don't accept it. All programs have ways to block unwanted messages. If someone starts bothering you with IMs, don't waste time arguing with him or her. Instead, report the person right away to your ISP and your parents. You will have the satisfaction of knowing you have gotten the person in a lot of trouble, or maybe even kicked off his or her ISP.

Instant messaging can be fun. It gives you a chance to chat privately with one of your friends.

Unlike shopping at the mall, you can shop online at almost any time.

Chapter Four

Going Shopping

The Internet is a terrific place to shop. You can find just about anything anyone could ever want to buy or sell online, from books to shoes. Shopping on the Internet is like going to the mall without leaving your room. And you can go shopping even if there is a blizzard outside or you are sick at home.

Some things about shopping are the same, whether you are going shopping online or going shopping in a mall. First

Before you buy anything online, make sure you have your parents' permission.

of all, you need money to shop. Naturally, you should never use your parents' credit cards without their permission. That would get you into trouble with them. What is more, remember that it's also illegal to use someone else's credit card without permission. But suppose that your parents do give you

Typing the Stores

"Brick and mortar" is the term for a company in an actual building—one with walls made up of bricks and mortar, for example. A business that has no real store is called a virtual store. A business that has both an actual building and a web store is called a "click-and-mortar" store. The "click" refers to the click of the computer mouse.

permission to use their credit card—up to a certain amount. Now that you have the money, where are you going to shop? Your parents may be wondering if it is really safe to shop online. You can reassure them that some stores are as safe as, and maybe even safer than, any brick-and-mortar store.

Safe Shopping

What makes shopping online safe is that well-established online stores have Internet security systems in place, making it very difficult for anyone to steal your personal information, such as your credit card number. Many other online stores also have security systems, but not every store does. Look for a security system logo—for instance, a **glyph**, or symbolic picture, of a lock. If you don't see one anywhere on your computer screen, don't shop there.

This is one symbol that indicates a site has secure shopping.

How Secure Shopping Works

When you enter a credit card number on a secure site, a technology such as Secure Sockets Layer (SSL) puts the number into code the instant you send it. This way, even if some would-be thief does manage to get hold of your credit card number in the instant of transmission, the data is encoded and useless to him or her. Once the number is safely in the store's computer, it is decoded by the store, and your purchase is made.

It is also important to be certain that the store is genuine. There have been cases of fake stores, which are like the false fronts of buildings on a Hollywood movie set. They look real, but they have nothing behind them. These fake stores trick people into spending money on items that do not exist, or that will never be delivered. Look for a real street address and phone number somewhere on the site. If there is a phone number but no street address, or if there's nothing at all but an e-mail address, the whole thing may be a scam.

Online Auctions

Another way to shop is through online auctions. These virtual auctions work in much the same way as real auctions do. You look at the item listed for auction and type in a bid. At the end

of the auction, the item is sold to the person who placed the highest bid.

The biggest and most popular online auction site is eBay, which handles everything from bubble gum cards to fine art, but there are dozens of others. Some of them handle only specific items, such as hardware or appliances, while others specialize in art.

Auctions can be a lot of fun. You can hunt for a book you have always wanted to read, or get into the excitement of

Participating in an online auction takes self-control. You don't want to bid more than you can afford.

A Real Case of Auction Fraud

On March 26, 2001, two men in New Jersey were charged by a state grand jury with stealing more than $160,000 from thirty-nine people. They advertised computer equipment for sale at various Internet auction sites, received payment, but then never delivered the products. Such a fraud can earn a thief up to twenty years in jail. In this case, which was settled on May 2, 2002, the men got off easy. They were fined $10,000 and barred from using online auctions. It could have been much worse.

bidding against someone who wants the same item. It is fun as long as you have enough willpower. Before you start bidding on something, set yourself an upper limit, the highest amount that you are willing to spend. Stay with that limit, even if you have to write it down on a note and stick it right there on your computer screen to remind yourself! Make sure you don't catch auction fever. This isn't a real sickness. You have auction fever when you get so swept up by the excitement of a bidding war that you forget all about your upper limit, and keep placing higher and higher bids. You don't want to wind up buying something for more money than you have. You can't just back out and say, "I was only joking," either. Once you have agreed to buy something, you have to do just that. Your parents might

For Sale?

Some very strange things have turned up on the auction sites. One man offered to sell one of his kidneys and was arrested. He didn't seem to know that it is illegal in the United States to sell human body parts. Another man tried to sell his soul. He must have been very disappointed when no one wanted to buy it.

agree to bail you out, but they won't be happy about it.

On the other hand, you may fully intend to pay for whatever you win. Make sure that there is a guarantee either from the seller or, even better, from the auction site itself that you will get what you bid on. Not everything that is being offered for auction really exists.

Online auctions are also great places to get rid of things you don't want anymore. Suppose you have an *X-Men* comic from the 1990s that is a duplicate in your collection. You can put it up for sale on an auction site very easily. Just follow the guidelines posted on the site. Understand that the auction site will ask for a small fee (as little as twenty-five cents) and take a small percentage of the final bid. If you or your parents know how to use a scanner or a digital camera, you can even post a photo of the comic's cover. But be prepared: If the comic doesn't sell, you don't get the fee back. And if it does sell, even if the final price is lower than the one you wanted, you must send the comic to the winner as soon as you receive his or her money.

Online auction might be a good way for you to get rid of something you don't want anymore, such as a comic book.

43

In a city without laws, the streets would be deserted and businesses would be closed.

Chapter Five

The Rules of Netiquette

Every society, whether it is a country, a club, or the Internet, has to have its rules. Rules help each society regulate itself. Imagine a city without laws or rules. Drivers might go through red lights or not stop at stop signs. Businesses might fail because there are no laws against shoplifters. People could also rob each other because there are no laws against stealing. There have to be laws if a society is to run smoothly.

Play by the Rules

Read the terms of service agreement for your Internet account to learn the rules.

On the Internet, you may feel totally anonymous and beyond the reach of the law, but this is not the case. No user is untraceable. A skilled computer user can find out who has sent a message. You are responsible for what you write. There are

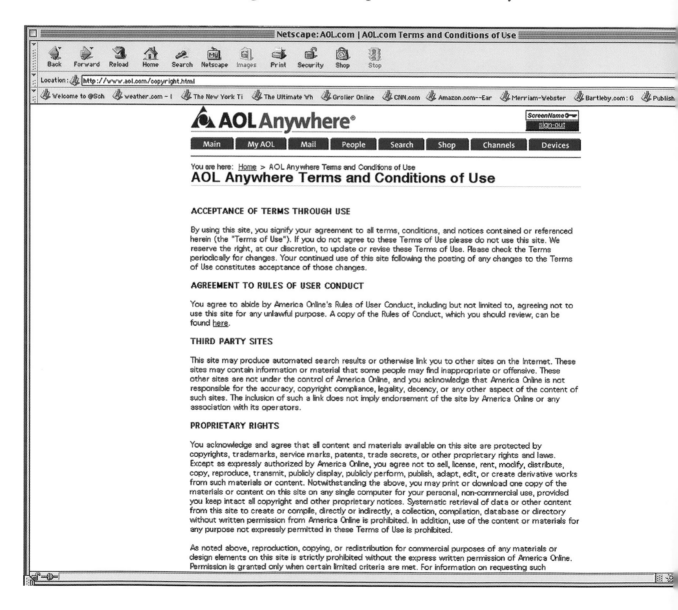

also rules that your ISP has set up. These are called terms of service, which are usually abbreviated as TOS. One TOS might say that no one can swear online. Another might warn that no user is allowed to send threatening e-mails to anyone. If you break one or more of the TOS for the first time, you will probably get a warning. But if you continue to break them, your ISP can legally deny you access to the Internet. Moreover, if you break some of the TOS, you are also breaking the law. For instance, it is a federal crime to send threats through the mail. That extends to e-mail as well.

Think before you send messages. You may only be joking when you send an e-mail to someone, "Do that again, and I'll beat you up," but the other person may not realize that it's a joke. You could be in big trouble with your ISP, and maybe with your parents as well. And never, even as a joke, tell someone that you are going to shoot or kill anyone. Not only is this never funny, at the very least, it could get you banned by your ISP and worse. It could even get you arrested.

A society is made up of more than just its laws. There are also rules of courtesy. Courtesy is more than saying "please" and "thank you" although that's part of it. Courtesy is also holding the door for someone with an armload of packages or giving up a seat on a bus to someone with crutches. You could live in a world without courtesy, but you probably would not like it.

The Internet community has its rules of courtesy too. Etiquette means good manners. Good etiquette on the Internet is

There are many ways to be courteous, such as helping someone carry groceries.

called **netiquette**. No one is sure who first coined the word, but netiquette means showing the proper online courtesy to others.

Some of the rules of netiquette are the same as in the real world. Calling someone stupid or ugly is just as hurtful online as it would be if you said it to someone's face. And, as noted above, it's not just rude, but downright illegal to try scaring or

Naming Names

The term "**flame war**," which means an online fight, comes from a character in *X-Men* comic books.

The Human Torch, a superhero, would start his fire while shouting the words "Flame on!"

threatening someone online just as it would be if you did it in person. Insulting someone online is a really good way to start a flame war. A flame war is an online fight. Some flame wars can be very nasty, leaving everybody feeling bad. Netiquette frowns on them.

Expressing Yourself

It is difficult to express the feelings behind your words over the Internet because your message only appears as letters on a computer screen. Internet users have invented a series of symbols, called emoticons to deal with the problem. The word "emoticon" is a combination of two words, "emotion" and "**icon**," or picture. An emoticon, literally, is a picture of an emotion. It is added to the end of a sentence to show the emotions the writer wants to convey.

Here's a brief list of some of the most common emoticons:

:)	Smile
;)	Wink
:(	Frown
:p	Sticking out your tongue
<g>	Grin

Acronyms are words created by combining the first letters of a phrase. For instance, FBI stands for Federal Bureau of Investigation. In the Internet world, acronyms also help get emotions across.

Here's an example of some of the most common acronyms:

BTW	By The Way
IMHO	In My Humble Opinion
LOL	Laughing Out Loud
ROFL	Rolling On the Floor Laughing

Remembering to use emoticons and acronyms really makes online life easier for everyone. You get familiar with them pretty quickly. And you will know you have really become a **netizen**—a citizen of the Internet—when you find yourself using emoticons when you are not online!

Another netiquette rule is never send a message typed all in capital letters JUST LIKE THIS. That is read as shouting, and it simply is not polite. A message typed all in capital letters is also more difficult to read. If you want your messages to be read, you don't want to fool around with the way they look. If the letters look clear, without anything fancy about them, everyone will be happy to read what you have to say. If your messages are difficult to read, what you have to say is probably going to be ignored.

There are other things you can do to be a good netizen. You can refuse to vandalize websites. What does this mean? You have probably seen graffiti scrawled on walls or maybe a window someone has broken for no reason. That is **vandalism**. Online, some people think that it's funny or clever to change or ruin the programming code on a site so that the site

Just as the walls of buildings can be messed up by paint, some web pages are destroyed by vandalism.

doesn't look the way it should or doesn't work properly. But it is not funny at all to the person who may have spent hours building the site.

You can also refuse to plagiarize. **Plagiarism** is passing off someone else's work as your own. Maybe you have already seen something like this happen at school. A student copies an

The Internet can be a fun and exciting place to explore and learn.

article from a newspaper or encyclopedia and hands it in as his or her own writing. It is really easy to do this sort of thing on the Internet because you can cut and paste with a few clicks of the mouse. But just because it is easy doesn't make it right. You are still stealing from someone, after all.

What about those websites that offer to sell you term papers you can use in school? Even if you can afford the prices, the papers are not going to do you any good. For one thing, teachers know about those sites too. And teachers can usually tell if a paper is not written in a student's usual style of writing.

Here is another problem. Suppose that you are surfing the Internet and you see someone else's web page. It has a really cool look. You are in the middle of building your own home page and could easily copy the design. There wouldn't be a teacher to catch you at it. The rules of netiquette say, "Don't do it." Stealing is, after all, still stealing. Besides, what happens if the creator of the original site sees your copy? Why make an enemy out of someone who might have turned into a friend? Instead of stealing a design, why not e-mail the site's creator to say how cool you think it is and ask him or her how it was built?

What does this have to do with Internet safety? Netiquette is more important than you may realize. Following the rules of netiquette not only makes you a good netizen, but also prevents you from angering others and keeps you out of trouble.

The Internet is a wonderful place to visit. Just remember the rules of the Internet world, and you'll be sure to have a good time.

Glossary

acronym—a word created by combining the first letters of a phrase

computer virus—a software program deliberately designed to harm someone else's computer system

flame war—an online argument

glyph—a symbolic picture, such as a stick figure of a human being, that has a meaning

guarantee—a promise that something is as it is described

icon—a picture

Internet Service Provider—a company that gives customers access to the Internet

legitimate—true or honest

netiquette—the rules of online courtesy, a combination of the words "Net" and "etiquette"

netizen—a person who is at home on the Internet. It is a combination of the words "Net" and "citizen."

plagiarism—copying of someone else's work and claiming that it's your own

privacy—the state of being free from illegal prying or intrusion

spam—in Internet terms, junk e-mail

vandalism—in Internet terms, changing or ruining the code on someone else's website so that it doesn't look the way it should or doesn't work at all

web server—a computer with special software that stores web page files and communicates with a user's browser when these pages are requested

worm—a type of software program designed to harm computer systems. It is related to a computer virus.

To Find
Out More

Books

Dougherty, Karla. *The Rules to Be Cool: Etiquette and Netiquette.* Berkeley Heights, NJ: Enslow Publishers, 2001.

Gelman, Robert B. *Protecting Yourself Online: The Definitive Resource on Safety, Freedom, and Privacy in Cyberspace.* New York: HarperCollins, 1998.

Gralla, Preston. *Online Kids: A Young Surfer's Guide to Cyberspace.* New York: John Wiley & Sons, 1999.

Gregory, Callie. *Jeeves, I'm Bored: 25 Internet Adventures for Kids.* Emeryville, CA: Ask Jeeves, 2000.

———. *Jeeves, I Need Help!: Tips and Tricks for Kids on the Net.* Emeryville, CA: Ask Jeeves, 2000.

Mintzer, Richard, et al. *The Everything Kids Online Book: E-Mail, Pen Pals, Live Chats, Home Pages, Family Trees, Homework, and Much More!* Avon, MA: Adams Media Corporation, 2000.

Raatma, Lucia. *Safety on the Internet.* Minnetonka, MN: Bridgestone Books, Capstone Press, 1999.

Rothman, Kevin F. *Coping With Dangers on The Internet: A Teen's Guide To Staying Safe Online.* New York: Rosen Publishing, 2000.

Schwartau, Winn. *Internet & Computer Ethics for Kids: (and Parents & Teachers Who Haven't Got a Clue.)* New York: John Wiley & Sons, 1999.

Trumbauer, Lisa. *Free Stuff for Kids on the Net.* Brookfield, CT: Millbrook Press, 1999.

Organizations and Online Sites

Ask Jeeves
http://www.ajkids.com
This online site is a version of the AskJeeves.com search engine that is designed especially for young people.

Cookie Central
http://www.cookiecentral.com

This online site is a good source of information about cookies.

Federal Bureau of Investigation
http://www.fbi.gov/kids/6th12th/6th12th.htm
This government website has a special section for young people.

Internet Safety
http://www.worldkids.net/school/safety/internet
This online site offers some good tips about Internet safety.

Junk Busters
http://www.junkbusters.com
This online site is devoted to online privacy.

National Aeronautics and Space Administration
http://www.nasa.gov
This is one of the best sites to visit to see live space activity.

Spam Cop
http://spamcop.net
This online site is dedicated to getting rid of junk e-mail.

Yahooligans
http://www.yahooligans.com
This online site is a version of the Yahoo! search engine for young people.

A Note on Sources

Both the Internet and printed books were of great use in the writing of this book. Among the most useful of the numerous websites I consulted were http://kidsinternet.about.com/mbody/, which is a listing of sites for kids, and http://www.yahooligans.com, the kids-only version of the Yahoo.com search engine. Also useful was http://spamcop.net, which is an important anti-spam site and http://www.junkbusters.com, one of the better sites devoted to online privacy.

Among the many books available on the subject of Internet safety, some of the most useful were Karla Dougherty's *The Rules to Be Cool: Etiquette and Netiquette*, Preston Gralla's *Online Kids: A Young Surfer's Guide to Cyberspace*, and Robert B. Gelman's *Protecting Yourself Online: The Definitive Resource on Safety, Freedom, and Privacy in Cyberspace.*

—*Josepha Sherman*

Index

Numbers in *italics* indicate illustrations.

About The Author

Josepha Sherman is an author, editor, and professional folklorist. For Franklin Watts, she has written two other Watts Library titles, *The History of the Personal Computer* and *The History of the Internet*. She has also written several biographies on important people in computing and the Internet, including *Bill Gates: Computer King*, *Jeff Bezos*, and *Jerry Lang and David Philo: Chief Yahoos*. Ms. Sherman has authored more than forty novels, including fantasy and science fiction titles.